W9-DEF-988

My Brother Otto
and the Birthday Party

My Brother Otto
and the Birthday Party

Meg Raby

Illustrations by **Elisa Pallmer**

GIBBS SMITH
TO ENRICH AND INSPIRE HUMANKIND

One more sleep until it's Saturday—our friend Ruthie's birthday party! I picked out the prettiest dress to wear!

I told Otto he could wear his new **blue** shirt, but he hid it under all of his other shirts. Otto LOVES yellow— not **blue**.

Otto is nonspeaking, and he moves his whole body
and uses his tablet to say what he's feeling.

Mom takes us to pick out a present for Ruthie.
I find a new art set full of paints and glitter.

Otto runs to where the music is. He picks out music with a dragon on the cover for Ruthie.

Each time he and Ruthie play together, they go outside and jump. Ruthie always jumps with her dragon stuffie. She talks about dragons a lot.

They take turns picking out music to jump to, too. Sometimes they do this until it's time for dinner—they have so much fun together.

Otto is so good at picking out gifts. Dad says this is because Otto connects objects and activities with people he loves.

Before bedtime, Mom tells me to show Otto pictures of other birthday parties we've been to. This will help him be ready for tomorrow.

Mom says it's Otto's own way of understanding things—it's like instead of his ears he uses his eyes to understand.

Mom also reminded me that birthday parties have a lot of stuff going on—that ALL our senses are at work! There are many sights, sounds, and smells to take in. Otto is autistic, and he experiences birthday parties in his own way.

After breakfast, I put on my dress and my new headband from Grandma. Otto gets dressed and puts on his earphones that make things quiet.

Otto wears his earphones because things sound extra loud to him—and birthday parties can be very, VERY loud.

When we get to the party, I give Ruthie her present. She doesn't look right at me, but she smiles and says hello. Like Otto, Ruthie can get overwhelmed. It's easier for her to say what she wants to say when she's not looking at people's faces.

Otto runs up to the bubble machine and flaps his wings. Flapping is how Otto shows he is excited. And bubbles? Otto really likes bubbles!

Dad says this is because Otto can see magic we can't. There must be a lot of magic in those bubbles—he's been over there for a long time!

Sometimes I wish I could see what he sees. For now, I think he might want to be left alone. Sometimes Otto feels his best when he gets time to be by himself.

At cake time we sing "Happy Birthday."

It's a good thing Otto has his earphones on. He even brought Ruthie hers. She doesn't like when things get too loud, either.

Since Otto doesn't talk and doesn't sing, he uses the pictures and words on his tablet to say what he needs to say. He takes out his tablet and has the happy birthday song play from it.

Otto loves music and he especially loves cake time at birthday parties.

I take the first piece Ruthie's mom offers me. They're all huge! But Otto looks the cake up and down to find his perfect piece—one with yellow icing or yellow sprinkles.

I'm pretty sure all other colors must be too much for Otto. I wonder if they make his head hurt. I wouldn't like other colors either if they hurt my head.

If there's no yellow on it Otto won't eat the cake. Who would want to go to a birthday party and not eat cake?

During present time, Otto lines each one up across the floor. He even does it by size! He likes things to be nice and neat. Ruthie tells me she loves her new art set. This makes me feel good.

When she opens up Otto's gift, she starts flapping and jumping up and down. She even squeals. Otto joins her. He grabs his tablet and pushes these buttons: Dragon + Music + for + Jumping!

Ruthie goes up to Otto and puts her forehead on Otto's forehead.

Ruthie's mom told me this is a way that Ruthie shows she is very thankful for something or someone.

Mom comes inside and tells us we'll be going home in ten minutes. Otto sets the timer on his tablet. Otto likes to know when something is going to change so he can be ready.

The timer goes off. Ruthie gives us our party favors and hands a yellow balloon to Otto. She begins to rock back and forth.

Otto starts flapping his wings again. They both are very happy.

I am very happy, too.

Even though Otto and I experienced the party differently, we both had a great time. And everyone was glad he came!

And look at him! He loved it!

First Edition

26 25 24 23 22   5 4 3 2 1

Text © 2022 Meg Raby
Illustrations © 2022 Elisa Pallmer

All rights reserved. No part of this book may be reproduced by any means
whatsoever without written permission from the publisher,
except brief portions quoted for purpose of review.

Published by
Gibbs Smith
P.O. Box 667
Layton, Utah 84041

1.800.835.4993 orders
www.gibbs-smith.com

Designed by Elisa Pallmer
Manufactured in Kyunggi-do, Korea in May 2022 by Pacom Communications

Gibbs Smith books are printed on either recycled, 100% post-consumer waste,
FSC-certified papers or on paper produced from sustainable PEFC-certified forest/controlled wood source.
Learn more at www.pefc.org.

Library of Congress Control Number: 2022930965
ISBN: 978-1-4236-6141-2